SCOUTING
FOR CLUES

SCOUTING FOR CLUES

BRANDI DOUGHERTY
ILLUSTRATED BY PAIGE POOLER

Andrews McMeel
PUBLISHING®

CHAPTER 1

BARK PARK

THE MISSING BLUEBERRIES

Scout was in a good mood. The weather was still crisp, but spring was in the air, and she was headed to Bark Park. Not only that, but her human had taken her to the farmers' market yesterday and he'd bought three containers of fresh blueberries! Scout had even gotten to sample a couple while they were there. She'd reported with a happy bark that they were delicious.

Scout's human unlatched the park's front gate, and Scout pushed it open with her nose. Her human set Scout's bowl of blueberries on the usual bench before heading over to greet the other people near the water fountain.

Scout looked longingly at her

blueberries for a minute but decided to stick to her routine: she'd take a lap around the park to say hi to her friends and make sure there were no mysteries to be solved. Then she'd come back to the bench and enjoy her snack.

Walter was sitting by the fence, scratching behind his ear.

Rocky sat nearby, eyeing Walter nervously.

"I've been hearing these little squeaking noises all morning," Rocky said, shifting from paw to paw. "Though it's not really a squeak. It's more of a . . . a chirping sound."

"No way!" Walter stopped scratching. "I've been hearing it too! I thought I had something stuck in my ear, but if you are hearing it, then it must be something else."

Scout walked over to them and listened for the sound. "Huh. I don't hear anything."

"I think it may have stopped," Rocky said. "It was probably nothing. At least I hope it was nothing . . ."

Scout chuckled. "I'll keep my ears open, just in case."

Scout spied Maggie coming into the park with a rope toy dangling from her mouth. Just behind her, Sprinkles was barking impatiently, wanting to enter.

Once they were both inside the park, they headed right for Gus, who was sitting under a tree and chewing on a bone. Scout made her way over to join them.

"Hi there, Scout," Gus said.

"That looks like a good bone, Gus." Scout smiled. The bone reminded her of her own treat waiting on the bench.

She decided that everything in the park was as it should be. All of her friends were there, and no mysteries needed solving. Scout was a little bit disappointed—she loved a good mystery. But she was also happy that she'd get to plop down and enjoy her blueberries for a while.

Scout strolled back over to her

bench, but something made her stop in her tracks. She looked left and right. Her blueberries were *gone!* She scanned the park and found her human. He was still talking to the other people near the water fountain, and his hands were empty. So where were her blueberries?

Scout gasped. There *was* a mystery at the park today—her own!

Rocky sensed Scout's distress and came trotting over. "Scout, what's wrong?" he asked, sounding nervous.

"My blueberries are gone!" Scout said rather loudly.

Scout wasn't one to get upset unnecessarily, but this was a pretty big deal.

Soon all of the other dogs were gathered around. Scout hopped up on the bench to address the crowd. "My human put my blueberries on this bench when we arrived. But now they're gone. Has anyone seen them?"

A murmur went through the group. All of the dogs shook their heads or barked no.

Scout knew just what to do. She walked to the front gate to retrace the steps she had taken

when she had come into the park. She kept her eyes wide open and her nose on high alert as she walked slowly from the gate to the bench. She circled the bench, looking at it from all sides, but she saw no sign of the blueberries.

"What do you think happened, Scout?" Maggie asked, bouncing up to her.

But Scout wasn't ready to start guessing. She had a theory that she wanted to investigate first. "Let's talk to Tippy," Scout said, spotting the plump squirrel on the ground near Gus. Tippy was always scrounging around for dropped dog treats or other food in the park.

Tippy was holding something small and round in her paws. Scout stopped in front of the squirrel and sat down. "What are you eating, Tippy?" she asked, her fawn-colored ears twitching a bit as she spoke. The other dogs gathered by Scout.

"An acorn," Tippy replied with

her mouth full. She held out the nut, and Scout could see where she'd been nibbling on it.

"Have you had any other treats this afternoon?" Scout continued, tapping her back paw on the dirt.

Tippy shrugged. "I found half

a Pooch Puff over by the gate and a few crackers at the playground next door. Why?"

Scout stood, inching closer to Tippy. "What about blueberries?"

Tippy dropped what was left of the acorn and looked at Scout. "Not today. Why? Do you have some?"

"I did, but now they're all missing!" Scout squeaked. "Are you sure you haven't seen them?"

Tippy looked a little nervous. "Scout, you know that I have

helped myself to a blueberry or two from time to time, but usually only if you drop one. And
I would never take them all!"

Gus pushed through the line of dogs and cleared his throat. A line of drool hung from his flappy jowls. "She's telling the truth, Scout. Tippy's been working on that acorn for a while now. She was on the branch above me when you said hello earlier."

Scout's ears relaxed a little bit. "Thanks, Gus," she said. "Sorry, Tippy. I'm just checking all of the possibilities."

"That's okay, Scout," Tippy replied.

Scout wasn't sure what to do next. While she thought, she heard a faint chirping sound in the wind—just like what Walter and Rocky had described. But that mystery would have to wait. The blueberries were still missing, and they were her top priority!

Scout decided to put her nose to the dirt and look for more clues. She sniffed around the base of a tree and then started back toward the bench, trying to pick up the scent of the blueberries. Halfway there, she found three stray blueberries in the grass. She pushed them around with her nose. Someone hadn't taken the

time to pick up every blueberry, so they must have grabbed them in a hurry. Scout would have eaten the abandoned blueberries, but they were evidence.

Scout continued her survey of the park. She sniffed around the water fountain and over to the hole in the back fence, and then she circled back to the front gate and ended up next to the bench again. Suddenly she stopped, sniffed the air, and listened. She heard Abigail let out a loud caw.

Scout hurried to the base of the tree where Tippy had just finished her acorn. Scout scanned the tree and her eyes landed on Abigail's nest, high up and partially hidden in the branches. She squinted, looking closer. Then she listened. She looked down at the ground and noticed that she was standing right next to the fallen blueberries she had found earlier. Scout smiled. "I think I know what happened," she announced.

The other dogs, many of whom

had been watching her investigate around the park, stopped what they were doing to listen.

Scout took another step toward the tree. She was going to call to Abigail, but her voice cracked and she hiccupped instead. She had to clear her throat and start again. "Abigail!" Scout barked. "Your babies have hatched!"

The big crow peered down from the tree, bobbing her head. "Yes, last night!"

"Congratulations!" Scout called. "Did they enjoy my blueberries?"

Several dogs gasped.

"Abigail took the blueberries?" Rocky asked.

Scout nodded. "She fed them to her babies. Right, Abigail?"

Abigail cawed loudly. "I did. The chicks were so hungry that I grabbed the first food I saw. Sorry, Scout. I'll remember to ask next time."

Scout wagged her tail. By examining the clues—the chirps and the fallen berries—she was happy to have solved another mystery. *And,* she thought, *I have two more containers of blueberries at home to look forward to!*

CHAPTER 2

BARK PARK

THE LEASHED PUPPY

As soon as her human closed the gate behind them, Scout bounded to the middle of the park, where a group of dogs was gathered in a circle. *Something's going on!* Scout wound her way between Maggie's and Rocky's legs to get to the center. There, Scout saw a puppy! By the looks of her, she was a black lab, with big paws and soft, floppy ears. She wore a pink collar attached to a very long leash that was tied around the trunk of a tree. Scout thought that was strange. Dogs didn't usually wear leashes in the park.

The other dogs in the circle were barking question after question at the puppy, and she was lying on her belly with a paw over her face. *She's shy*, Scout

thought, approaching the puppy carefully. "Hi, I'm Scout," she said. "What's your name?"

"I'm Lulu," the little puppy whispered. "It's my first day here."

"Welcome, Lulu!" Scout barked more loudly, so the other dogs could hear her name. "Everybody's friendly at Bark Park. You have nothing to worry about. We're just excited because it's not every day that we get to meet a new pal!"

Slowly, Lulu lowered her paw

and stood up. She looked around at all of the smiling faces.

Maggie stepped forward and dropped her new red ball on the grass in front of Lulu. "Want to share my ball today?"

Lulu beamed. "I'd love to!" She pawed at the ball and then darted forward. The only problem was that her leash was still tied to the tree. Lulu was stopped short as the ball rolled out of reach.

"Can someone please unclip me? I want to run around!" Lulu whined.

"Why didn't your human take off your leash?" Scout asked.

Lulu tilted her head and said, "I dunno." She gave a quick scratch and then dashed left and right, testing the length of her leash.

"Maybe they forgot," Rocky said.

"Maybe," Scout agreed, smiling. They had a mystery on their paws! Why was Lulu on her leash *inside* the park? And how could they set her free? There were *two* mysteries! Scout inspected the leash clipped to Lulu's collar. It was different from her own leash. "Anyone know how to unclip this type of

leash?" she asked the crowd.

A couple of dogs stepped forward to look but then shook their heads. "Not that one."

Lulu whined again and scratched at the clip, her eyes darting back and forth.

As Scout inspected the leash more closely, Walter strolled over. "What's going on here?" he asked.

Scout pointed her nose at the

new puppy. "This is Lulu. We're not sure why she's still wearing her leash. Can you get it off?"

Lulu's eyes grew wide as Walter stepped toward her. She looked down nervously. Walter nudged the leash clip with his nose. "Sorry, kid. Don't have much

experience with leashes. I've never been on one!"

"Good point," Scout said. "Who else might be able to help?"

Rocky backed away. "Not me!" he said. "After wearing the cone of shame for so long, I don't want to get tangled up in anything!" Rocky had worn a wide plastic funnel around his neck while an injury on his paw had healed. He never wanted to do that again!

"Wait a second! That leash looks familiar," Maggie said,

practically bouncing up and
down. Scout wagged her tail. She
knew the Goldendoodle was eager
to get Lulu off her leash so they
could play ball together.

"This was my favorite type of leash. Every morning, after my human went to work, I practiced opening the clip. It took me a whole week to figure it out. But once I did, I could unclip it really fast! My human was so confused. But when she realized what I could do, she bought a different kind." And with that, Maggie flicked a front paw at the clasp, and it dropped to the ground. Lulu stared at the fallen leash for about two seconds before she

bounded out of the circle of dogs and ran. And ran and ran.

Scout and her friends turned to watch as the puppy darted around the park, churning up dust.

Just then, Scout saw two things happen at once and her heart thumped in her chest. "Oh no!" she whispered. Sprinkles and his human had entered the front gate of Bark Park right as Lulu ran in their direction.

The gate was still closing when Lulu scurried through the opening and onto the street. The other dogs gasped.

"What was that?" Sprinkles huffed as he trotted over.

"Our new friend, Lulu! It's her

first day at the park, and I'm not

sure she'll be able to find her way

back in," Scout said.

"Scout!" Rocky barked. "What

should we do?! What should we do?!"

"This is bad," Sprinkles said in his usual grumpy way. "This is *very* bad."

Scout saw her human talking to someone she didn't recognize at the bench. The person had a brand-new treat bag clipped to his belt. Scout realized that Lulu's leash had looked unused, too—no frayed edges or dirt on it yet. Scout guessed that the person was Lulu's human, and he must have just adopted her, since all of his supplies were new.

The humans hadn't realized what had happened yet, so it was up to Scout and her friends to get Lulu back. "Okay," Scout said. "We have to act fast. Maggie and Rocky, you try to get the humans' attention. Maybe they'll realize Lulu is missing and come to help. In the meantime, Sprinkles and I will use the loose board at the back of the fence to sneak out and go after Lulu."

Maggie and Rocky rushed toward Lulu's human. They both barked and hopped in a circle. Scout and Sprinkles ran for the back fence. Walter joined them there, agreeing to keep watch in case Lulu ran his way.

Scout and Sprinkles hurried through the alley and toward the main street. "Hey! Where are you running off to?" Judy, the stray alley cat, asked from her perch on top of a garbage can.

"Runaway puppy!" Sprinkles called back to her.

"I just saw a flash of black fur pass the end of the alley!" Judy shouted after them.

"Thanks, Judy!" Scout said. "That's probably her!"

Out on the sidewalk, Scout looked right and left. She spotted Lulu on the corner of a very busy intersection, leaning against a garbage can. Scout ran toward her frightened new friend, and Sprinkles followed. "Lulu!" Scout barked when they were close.

"Help!" Lulu cried. The poor pup was shaking.

Scout put her paw on Lulu's back. "It's okay. Follow us. We'll

take you back to your human at
the dog park."

Lulu nodded and let out a
small whimper. She followed
Scout and Sprinkles back down

the street and through the alley. Walter held the loose fence board aside so they could all squeeze through. As soon as Scout, Sprinkles, and Lulu got to the tree Lulu's leash was tied to, Rocky and Maggie stopped barking and ran to meet them. All of the humans looked very confused, but then Lulu's human rushed over and scooped her up. "You clever pup! How did you get this off?" he asked as he clipped the leash back onto Lulu's collar.

Scout breathed a sigh of relief. "I don't think Lulu's human forgot to take off her leash," she told the other dogs. "He knew Lulu would run without it, and he didn't want her to get into any trouble. Next time I'll trust that the leash is there for a reason." All the dogs agreed. And now that their new friend was safe, they stretched out in the grass to recover from all the excitement.

I'm glad we solved the mystery, but I'm even more glad that Lulu is okay and has a human who looks out for her, Scout thought as she settled in for a much-needed nap.

CHAPTER 3

BARK PARK

THE MYSTERY MATERIAL

The morning air was a bit cool as Scout scanned Bark Park. Gus was in his favorite place under his favorite tree. He was already snoring away, his breathing sounding like a chain saw rumbling to life. Rocky was there, too, sniffing around the base of the tree and being careful not to disturb Gus.

Scout headed over to see Rocky while Maggie and Lulu bounded around the park, chasing a ball together. Maggie was thrilled when the puppy started coming to the park. Lulu was the only dog that could keep up with her. And now that Lulu had finished puppy school, she could finally enjoy the park without being on a leash.

"Hi, Scout!" Lulu called between tosses.

"Hiya, Schout!" Maggie said as she caught the ball in her mouth.

"Good morning!" Scout tipped her nose in their direction.

Just then, chattering at the fence caught everyone's attention. Tippy sat on the fence laughing in her own squeaky way. Below her, Walter, the local stray, was staring at the park entrance with wide eyes.

"What's so funny?" Rocky asked, looking a little nervous that Tippy might be laughing at him. He quickly ran a paw over his face to make sure nothing was stuck there.

"Look!" Walter pointed toward the gate. Scout and her friends all spun around to see what

could have Tippy so worked up and Walter so surprised.

Sprinkles was standing by the front gate, and the little terrier mix did not look happy. Not that he usually looked happy. His typical mood was grumpy, bordering on annoyed—but usually just grumpy. Today he looked grumpy *and* annoyed.

Scout squinted her eyes and walked slowly toward Sprinkles.

The other dogs followed as Tippy ran along the fence and then jumped down to the bench to grab a half-eaten dog treat there.

"What are you wearing?" Scout asked.

"I don't know," Sprinkles mumbled. Something was wrapped around the middle of his body and down his front legs.

Gus had woken up from his nap, and he was curious about the commotion. It took a minute for the old dog to get up, but eventually he strolled over to the group. "What's all the fuss about?" he asked.

"Sprinkles has a new . . . *thing* on, and we're trying to figure out what it is," Scout said as she stepped aside to give Gus a better view.

Maggie jumped into a pile of

leaves nearby just to hear them crunch. Then she shook the leaves out of her fur and ran back to the group. "Why are you wearing that, Sprinkles?" she asked, tilting her head to one side.

Sprinkles sighed, a low growl rumbling up from his chest. "I don't know *that,* either.

My human put it on me right before we left for the park. Well, first he had to wipe off the peanut butter that the little rascal had smeared on my back."

"You mean the toddler?" Scout smiled. Sprinkles lived with a 2-year-old human who loved him, but Sprinkles didn't exactly feel the same way.

"Toddler. Rascal. Same thing," Sprinkles grumbled. "Then my human put this *thing* on me and we left. No warning.

No explanation. No nothing. It's terrible!"

"Huh," Scout said. Just then her ears twitched. Wait a minute—this was *a mystery!* If Sprinkles didn't know what this strange thing was, then it was up to Scout to figure it out! Scout walked in a circle around Sprinkles, studying him from all angles. Thin strands of bright pink material were knit together and hugged Sprinkles around his back and across his tummy.

The woven material went up to his collar and about halfway down his front legs.

"What are those paper things stuck all over it?" Scout asked, nudging one with her nose.

"Stickers," he muttered into the grass.

"What are stickers?" Rocky asked, cocking one of his big ears.

"The toddler put them there. She has pages and pages of these little sticky papers with pictures on them. I don't know what

they're for, but she loves putting them on me."

"Interesting," Scout said as she finished her circle around Sprinkles.

Rocky stepped forward to inspect Sprinkles too. "Did you have to go to the vet? Maybe it's like my cone and it's to stop you from licking."

Scout smiled at her friend. "That is a really good guess,

Rocky," she barked. "I hadn't thought of that."

Sprinkles lifted his head from the ground just enough to shake it back and forth. "No. I haven't been to the vet since my checkup a while back. And I don't have any injuries."

Walter pushed away from where he'd been leaning against the fence. "I once met a dog that didn't have any fur. Maybe all your fur's falling out, like his did, and that's your new coat!"

Sprinkles said, grumpily, "My fur is *not* falling out, Walter!"

Scout's ears twitched. She thought about Walter's words. Just then the breeze picked up, sending more leaves twirling

down from the tree nearby.

Scout looked at the trees all around them, inside and outside the park. Many of their leaves were shades of bright red and orange. Other leaves were already brown and starting to fall. She licked at the air to test it. It tasted a bit like woodsmoke. Then she smiled and stood up a little taller. "I think I know what it is!" she announced to her friends.

"You do?" Rocky's eyes were wide. "What is it?"

Sprinkles lifted his head, looking interested but still annoyed.

Scout marched forward, but her front paw caught on a mound of dirt and she tripped, stumbling for a moment before regaining her balance. "Whoops!" she squealed. She walked over and stood next to Sprinkles. "Walter wasn't totally wrong. Not exactly."

"See?" Walter said, looking satisfied. Sprinkles scowled.

"Sprinkles isn't losing his fur,

but he is wearing a kind of coat. The weather's changing. It's getting colder and the leaves are falling from the trees," Scout said. Then she turned to Sprinkles and explained, "Your human wanted to keep you warm at the park. That's why he put it on you before you went outside. It's a . . . a . . . what are those things called?" Scout tilted her head, searching for the right word.

"It's a sweater," Gus said, his voice gruff with age. "Now I remember. I've seen a sweater or two in the past."

Scout wagged her tail. "Yes, that's the word! It's a sweater."

Gus said, "I knew it looked familiar. I remember one dog who wore a sweater every day during

the cooler months. One time a leaf got stuck in the back of the sweater and the dog thought a bird had landed on him. I've never seen a dog run in circles so fast."

All the dogs laughed—well, most of them did. Rocky nodded in sympathy for the poor dog.

Maggie rubbed her nose against the sweater. "It does feel nice and cozy," she said.

Sprinkles stood up. "My human must have noticed I was shivering in the park the last few

mornings. But now I'm toasty! Thanks for figuring it out, Scout." He wasn't grumpy anymore. In fact, he looked proud to be wearing his new sweater.

Scout nodded. "The reason for

the stickers, however . . . Well, that's a mystery for another day," she barked, wagging her tail as she walked over to her waiting bowl of blueberries.

WHAT DO CROWS EAT?

The dogs are surprised to learn that Abigail fed Scout's blueberries to her baby crows. While adult crows eat just about anything, including insects, small animals, nuts, and even garbage, baby crows need softer foods that their parents can feed them. Blueberries are perfect for them, and so are other fresh fruits like grapes, cranberries, and cherries.

Around the time crows learn to fly (usually a week or two after they hatch), they also start to feed themselves. That's when they try many different kinds of foods. But blueberries remain a good snack for crows—and people!

WHY DO DOGS NEED LEASHES?

When Lulu the puppy shows up at Bark Park, the other dogs help her get off her leash. They quickly learn why that's a bad idea when Lulu escapes!

Leashes do more than just keep dogs from running away. They prevent pets from jumping on people and other animals and keep them safe from moving cars. Leashes also help with dog training, which leads to healthier, happier dogs (and humans!).

Even though Lulu wants to be free of her leash, her human has good reasons for making her wear it. And when Lulu returns to Bark Park, the other dogs will leave her leash alone!

WHEN SHOULD DOGS WEAR CLOTHES?

Sprinkles is confused by his new sweater, and so are the other dogs at Bark Park.

While most dogs don't need jackets or sweaters to stay warm, they can help smaller dogs stay comfortable when it's cold out. Poodles, Chihuahuas, greyhounds, terriers, and other dogs with thin or short fur might even need them indoors sometimes.

But it's not a good idea to put clothes on dogs if it makes them uncomfortable or upsets them.

Clothes aren't just for cold weather. Booties can protect sensitive paws from hot sidewalks, and some dogs feel calmer wearing a snug-fitting shirt when loud noises from thunder or fireworks scare them.

ABOUT THE AUTHOR

Brandi Dougherty was born and raised in Kalispell, Montana. After earning an English degree at Linfield College, she spent eight years working in children's publishing at Scholastic before moving to California, where she pursued writing and freelance editing full-time. Brandi now calls sunny Los Angeles her home, where she wrangles two adorable kids and one crazy dog with her husband, Joe.

ABOUT THE ILLUSTRATOR

Paige Pooler has illustrated many books for kids, including *Liberty Porter, First Daughter* by Julia DeVillers and *Jim Henson's Enchanted Sisters*. Paige lives in sunny southern California where there are many lovely parks for her to visit with her two rescue dogs, Gracie and Freddie. Playing at the park is their favorite thing to do together!

Andrews McMeel Publishing
a division of Andrews McMeel Universal
1130 Walnut Street, Kansas City, Missouri 64106
www.andrewsmcmeel.com

Epic! Creations, Inc.
702 Marshall Street, Suite 280
Redwood City, California 94063
www.getepic.com

21 22 23 24 25 SDB 10 9 8 7 6 5 4 3 2 1

Paperback ISBN: 978-1-5248-6474-3
Hardback ISBN: 978-1-5248-6805-5

Library of Congress Control Number: 2020947818

Design by Dan Nordskog

Photo credits: page 85, carrion crow photo by John Hawkins/
FLPA/Minden Pictures
page 87, puppy photo by smit312/Shutterstock.com
page 89, Scottish terrier photo by WilleeCole Photography/
Shutterstock.com

Made by:
King Yip (Dongguan) Printing & Packaging Factory Ltd.
Address and location of manufacturer:
Daning Administrative District, Humen Town
Dongguan Guangdong, China 523930
1st Printing – 1/11/21